PALETTE OF THE IMPROBABLE

PALETTE OF THE IMPROBABLE

TALES OF HORROR & DARKNESS

STEVE VASQUEZ

.

Palette of the Improbable by Steve Vasquez

Published by: Steve Vasquez
Editing by: Steve Vasquez

10 9 8 7 6 5 4 3 2 1
1. Horror 2. Dark Stories 3. Science Fiction
First Edition
Printed in U.S.A.

To my mother, Gloria, who loved a good scare and always had words of encouragement and to my wife, Jennifer, whose support and understanding are always right on the mark.

Contents

God Works in Mysterious Ways 1

Baby in the Mirror 7

Don't Order That Doll!. 15

Good Night, Sleep Tight. 33

Final Audition 39

Through A Wormhole Darkly. 49

A Hand Is a Terrible Thing to Waste. 73

About the Author. 81

Acknowledgments

I would like to thank all my family and friends who spent time reading and sometimes re-reading my stories. I couldn't have made this exciting and fun journey without your help.

God Works in
Mysterious Ways

Twilight was casting its blurry mix of light and shadows across the living room. As Gabriel sat in his favorite rattan chair waiting for the record to play, he softly stroked the top of the rosewood hope chest, running his index finger across the length, feeling every indention, imperfection and deterioration, contemplating its contents. As he was deciding what treasure to enjoy first, the melodious harmonies of Los Tres Baladistas (The Three Balladeers) filled the room:

Hermosa mía, tú siempre estás aquí conmigo. Ni el espacio ni el tiempo alguna vez disminuira' nuestro amor.

The tune was sad and at the same time beautiful and it was one of Gabriel's favorites. Every note softly kissed his ears as if it were his first time hearing them, creating an aura of serenity. He was now in the mood to read aloud to his daughter. Gabriel turned the volume lower then scanned the day's newspaper, May 17, 1978, until he found an article that intrigued him. It was about how some grave robbers had stolen the body of silent film star, Charlie Chaplin, for ransom and how it had been recently recovered. He read out loud: "It was dug up from a field about a mile away from the Chaplin home in Corsier near Lausanne, Switzerland. Swiss police have arrested two men who have confessed to stealing the coffin and reburying it."

He looked up at his daughter who was lying on the sofa and laughed abruptly then stopped without really knowing why he did either. Gabriel continued reading, "Aldo Moro, former Italian Prime Minister has been kidnapped." He sighed heavily then put the paper down. "Elysa, the world is sometimes too strange and scary a place for me." He then raised his arm and swung his wrist from left to right with an imaginary baton (like the conductors he had seen conducting the bands in the dance halls of his youth) as his finger danced in unison with the tune. "A-a-ah, mija, now this is music." Enraptured in the moment, he serenaded along with the record, raising the volume of his voice as if The Three Balladeers and their instruments were his backup:

> *"Hermosa mía, tú siempre estás aquí conmigo. Ni el espacio ni el tiempo alguna vez disminuira' nuestro amor."*

> My beautiful one, you are always here with me. Neither space nor time will ever diminish our love.

He pulled out a pink hairbrush from the chest and held it up for Elysa to see. "¿Recuerdas este? "Remember this?" he joyously cried out. "It's the same one you've had since you were little. Your hair back then was so curly and thick." Her slight smile encouraged him to continue. "I remember you'd scream when your hair got caught in it. Mind if I brush it now?"

Gabriel smiled and without waiting for an answer knelt behind her, very carefully grasping her long hair from the ends then brushed slowly. When it suddenly stuck, he froze, expecting a window-shattering scream. But Elysa simply tilted her head backwards slightly with each new stroke and said nothing as if she silently approved. "You were so spoiled back then too, but how could I not spoil you after your mother left us?" The record continued to play:

> *Yo siempre te mantenga cerca y querido a mi corazón, mi hermoso sueño. Siempre serás conmigo. Nada nos puede separar.*

> I will always keep you near and dear to my heart, my beautiful dream. You will always be with me. Nothing can separate us.

"Aaah, mi flor, such powerful words, eh?" Next, he took a small wooden box out of the chest, opened it carefully, and removed some heliotropes wrapped in yellowed, tattered tissue. He tenderly sniffed the flowers and would swear before God that there remained a fragrance. The scent filled his nostrils and permeated every vein and blood cell with days past. He held the flowers up so she could see.

"These are from the summer you turned five. Remember? We traveled to Xochimilco to visit your grandmother. You became obsessed with riding the gondolas and we had such a hard time dragging you away from those floating gardens. Did I ever tell you how you got your nickname because of your love of flowers? Of course I did, mi flor. Probably hundreds of times. I'm getting old." Gabriel picked up his guitar and began to strum and sing along with the trio:

> *"Me volvería loco sin tu amor, mi sueño hermoso. Nunca vamos a estar separados."*

I'd go crazy without your love, my beautiful dream. We will never be apart.

The last song on side one ended and the hissing of the scratchy, old record lasted but a moment as Gabriel flipped it over to hear side two. A livelier tune began with a pizzicato of flamenco guitars. This instantly put a smile on the man whose face was aged well beyond its sixty years.

"Your mama thought this song was silly," he said, "but then again she was the more serious of the two of us. Listen to the vibrancy of the vocals. It brings the room to life—like being in the presence of a young woman in love." The feeling of young love momentarily preoccupied Gabriel's mind but was wrenched away, replaced with feelings of emptiness and loneliness. "What a shame you two barely knew each other. The doctors called it asbestosis." His pulse raced and perspiration begin to bead down his brow.

He turned away from his daughter and stared at a picture hanging on the drab olive wall: a photo of himself and Elysa at a local carnival. She's proudly holding a stuffed pink flamenco won by Gabriel for being the fastest at squirting water into a balloon and making it pop. Next to it hung another one of Gabriel and Juliana, his wife—both young and full of hope. The photos put him at ease and his heart stopped pounding through his chest. He glanced over at another photograph.

The frame was tarnished and the glass was web-cracked. It housed an image of Juliana, now older but with the same youthful smile. She was holding a plaque which read *Employee of the Year* and standing below a sign, *Southwest Textile Company*. "She loved her job," Gabriel continued. "She loved it for 12 years until it killed her." He looked over at Elysa for some sign of understanding, perhaps just a glint of compassion for his pain, but there was none. He grazed her cheek lovingly and exclaimed, "Ay, que' hermosa! How proud she would be to see how beautiful you turned out."

Carefully, he pulled out one more item from the chest: a brown teddy bear, now soiled and beaten with age, yet its brown eyes still retained their sparkle. "Recuerdes Tomas? Su mama compro esto. I believe she bought it soon after you were born. She knew you would need a companion since no other children could be around you. Funny how your mom and I were the same but different. She believed that God gives everyone just a little happiness on Earth but not too much so they could appreciate Heaven all the more. I believe there is never enough to go around, but we both loved you." The record had already ended but the words to the last song, *Love Without End*, echoed in his mind:

A pesar de que se han ido, nunca seremos separados y por lo que mi corazón llora hasta que yo ya no esté.

Even though you are gone, we will never be apart and so my heart cries on until I am no more.

Gabriel then took these last few moments to admire his daughter's beauty. He tenderly patted the sleeve of her white-laced gown, hoping that somehow she would awaken from her sleep, but she didn't for the gown was decrepit and tattered after twenty years of continual wear. Unfazed, Gabriel methodically slid his left arm under the golden eiderdown quilt that adorned her tiny body then did the same with his right, wrapping it around what should have been the legs of a full grown woman. Lifting her dehydrated, hardened form up with the ease one would lift an infant, he placed her in the wooden rosewood coffin along with the memorabilia of long ago.

He was about to close the lid when he noticed one more item sticking out from a corner inside the box. "I'd forgotten I gave this to you during our last visit. You must take better care of things," he said reprovingly. He positioned her fragile arms across her chest then pulled the handkerchief out and placed it gently inside her skeleton fingers so that they formed a cathedral-like enclosure around his monogrammed initials—G.O.D.—Gabriel Ortega Delgado. "Well, mi flor, it's time to sleep again," he said dreamily and closed the lid. Then Gabriel sat in the darkness and wept.

Baby in the Mirror

I was performing my duties as a night time orderly for the Metropolitan Hospital when I noticed the letter lying on the floor just outside room D-18. This was so unusual that at the end of my shift at 7:00 am I immediately took it to our Director, Dr. Tremain, for further instruction.

"Come in," he said. This was only the second time at Metropolitan that I'd been inside his office. The first being a month ago upon my arrival. "Jordan Balch, isn't it?" he asked. "Yes, sir," I replied.

"Well, Jordan, sit down, sit down. No need for formalities here. Ruth tells me you found a letter up on D wing." As I handed it to him, I wondered if I should have made an appointment with his secretary Ruth, first, rather than just dropping in. He peered down at it through thick reading glasses then smiled slightly. "Did you read it?" he asked.

"No, doctor. I brought it straight away." He handed it back to me.

"I want all my staff to be familiar with the patients they attend; therefore…" He motioned to the letter. I admit I was now very curious as to its contents. It read:

To Whom It May Concern,

I am writing this in the hope that you will fulfill my request to install a mirror in my room and here is why:

It was twenty years ago on the 23rd of September, 1946 when it all began. I remember the date because it was a week shy of our baby's second month. At the time, I was working on the line of a steel factory where the most deplorable of working conditions existed, but because I was in desperate need of extra income I committed to working double shifts for as long as they'd allow. My wife, Sondra, tragically had died during childbirth.

Fortunately, our neighbor, Mrs. Dorington, was willing to look after the baby while I worked and at the end of my second shift I'd return to care for him. Generally, Eugene was a happy baby but on this particular night, he was very cranky and would not go to sleep. His kicking and screaming was loud enough to wake the dead. I tried everything to get him to sleep: I sang to him, coddled him, rocked him back and forth and, I'm ashamed to say now, even got angry at him but nothing worked.

By 3:00 am I could barely keep my eyes open. It was at that time I happened to glance at the dresser mirror. I needed a distraction to take my mind off my exhausted state so I looked at myself directly in the eyes and asked, "Can you please do something with him?" To further the joke, I put our baby up against the mirror and smiled at myself for my foolishness. But I was fully-awakened when I suddenly felt the sensation that Eugene was being pulled away. It frightened me for a moment, but I felt comforted after looking down and seeing Eugene fast asleep. I looked up at my reflection and of course all I saw was myself smiling back and holding a sleeping baby. I put Eugene back in his crib and nodded off into a deep sleep.

I woke up convinced it was just a weird dream so I never mentioned it to anyone. The next day was Thursday, just two more days of work to go, but it was also a very long and tiring day. I returned home, hoping Eugene was in better spirits this night but it wasn't so. He was extra fidgety and after burping him, singing to him and pacing the floor for two hours, I was so exhausted, I'd forgotten about the night before, that is, until I glanced up at the mirror.

The longer I stared, the more it felt like my reflection and I were in two separate worlds, as if the mirror-me and his baby lived in another world, one with a calmer existence. The idea to offer my baby up to him again in the hope of getting a sleeping baby in return was attractive. I had at that point an overpowering sensation to let my mirror-me take control. I remember my mind felt numb, as if in a trance-like state, completely taken in by the idea of holding a quiet baby, longing for it, needing it. I held Eugene up to the mirror and again felt the pulling sensation. This time I wasn't afraid but thrilled that soon I'd be able to go to sleep. I don't remember paying much attention to Eugene after that but I must have set him down right away. I do remember glancing at my watch. It was 3:00 am. I woke up with a terrible headache and found I had not even changed out of my work clothes.

Friday was finally here. At the end of my shift, I was so happy to have the next two days off, I paid a co-worker 35 cents for a few shots of whiskey out of a bottle he kept in his car. But, my celebration was short-lived because, again, today, Eugene seemed determined to keep me from sleep. His crying was louder and even in the darkness, I could see his face getting red with frustration. The shots of liquor didn't help and I literally found myself falling asleep standing up.

I walked over to the mirror and didn't think twice about it. I put crying Eugene against the mirror and seconds later held calm Eugene. This time; however, things were different. The mirror-me was holding a baby who was still crying and wriggling about. He then walked the baby around the mirror image of the room as I stood still, frozen in shock because I could no longer see my true reflection. What I was seeing was myself doing things in the mirror that I know I wasn't doing. It was like watching myself in a movie. I realized then this was no reflection.

Although it looked like me and acted like me, this thing I was seeing was anything but me. After watching its movements for a few minutes, I was startled when it suddenly turned around and stared back at me with eyes that were glowing red. It smiled devilishly, showing off its sharp fangs, long-nailed claws and evil intent.

Was this an illusion, or worse, had I gone mad? I looked down at Eugene and he was still and peaceful but something was different. By now, the mirror-me had not only quieted its baby but was playing with him and making him laugh. By the moonlight that seeped into the room, I noticed something else. The baby I held in my arms was eerily still. I called out, "Eugene, Wake up! Daddy's here," but nothing happened. I shook him repeatedly in hopes of reviving him but with no success.

I screamed in horror when I realized what I held in my arms was dead. I had been tricked. By allowing this evilness access to Eugene, I had dropped my guard, letting it snatch Eugene and replace him with a dead baby. Where that poor dead child came from—what sad and horrible place—I don't know.

As the mirror-me walked over to the reflection of Eugene's crib and put my baby to bed, the image faded and became mere shadows of the night and I was once again staring at myself. Two days later a baby who looked like Eugene (but I'm convinced was not my son) was laid to rest. It was then I began to wonder why this thing decided to enter our world.

I recalled a few incidents, which at the time seemed unrelated. The first occurred before Eugene was born. My wife was cleaning the dresser mirror one day. She was in one of her cleaning moods and was particularly intent on removing a very stubborn smudge that would just not go away. As she applied pressure to this area, she swore to me later she saw her image flutter with an almost rippling effect like one sees when throwing a pebble in the water.

Another time after she was pregnant, I remember she was drinking a lot of water and sometimes she would leave half empty glasses on the dresser. As I was getting ready for work one morning, I saw the water in the glass shake, not once but three times. Granted, it was such an insignificant occurrence I soon forgot about it, but I know I wasn't imagining it.

Separately, these two incidents are unrelated, meaningless moments in one's life but looking back now, I see how they were indications that something unnatural was causing these things to happen. Could that thing have been watching us?...waiting for the right moment for us to be vulnerable.

As it turned out I was the one who gave it the chance it needed. You see, I believe my past had caught up with me. Growing up on a Navajo reservation where my family was entrenched in the ways shamanism, I had first-hand knowledge of things not of this world. I'd seen both my father and grandfather interact with otherworldly spirits in an effort to cleanse tribe members of their negative energy. Unfortunately, I was not as gifted in these ways and as a boy, my grandfather warned me about demons that lurked in the shadows, ready to prey on those who didn't know how to protect themselves from their destructive influences.

I'll admit now that after Sondra died, I began drinking excessively and was prone to indulge in immoral ways more than I should have. But why did it take my baby and why did it reveal itself to me? I could only come to the conclusion that there were unresolved conflicts between this spirit and my family ancestors. Because I lacked in this area, I shied away from the teachings of my people and was spiritually vulnerable to these evil powers. Perhaps it wanted to test me and determine if I was up to the challenge of resolving the past or perhaps it simply wanted to weaken me by stealing my most precious child. This is why I implore you to please allow a mirror in my room. I know I could lure back this entity and do whatever it takes to finally bring Eugene home. He's been away so long and I know he misses his father.

Sincerely,

Jeffrey (Ahiga) Sandoval

I looked up at Tremain with an empathy I'd not felt for any patient up to this time. He said nothing but walked over to a filing cabinet and pulled out a box. It contained a stack of letters, six inches thick. "The patient in D-18 has been here for twenty years now," he began, "and every couple of months, he writes a letter similar to if not exactly like the one you are holding and slips it under the door. Although, in this one, he left out how he became obsessed with the mirror, staring at for weeks non-stop in the hope of conjuring up his so called mirror man. As I understand it, he was in such a catatonic state when he was brought here and is considered mentally incompetent ever since. We allow the poor, lost man pen and paper whenever he asks. It's the least we can do."

"I am flabbergasted by this patient's story," I replied. "Do you think he really believes a mirror man exchanged his baby for a dead one?"

"I'm certain he believes it but in the years I've been here and the five before that, we've never put a mirror in his room. I see no reason to rile him up with false hope. From what I've found out through my research on this patient, Mr. Sandoval probably created his man in the mirror story as a way to cope with his baby's death."

Tremain handed me a copy of the latest American Medical Association Journal, dated July, 1966. "Perhaps you should read this," he said. "It may give you better insight into what this man went through. Poor Mr. Sandoval. If he only knew it wasn't his fault he might not have ended up here." I glanced down at the magazine. Just below our address *Metropolitan State Hospital, 300 Elm Street*, was the title *Sudden Infant Death Syndrome (SIDS), What We Know So Far*.

"There is one more thing, Jordan. You see, I've not been completely honest about this mirror business."

"How so, doctor?" I asked.

"Well, about fifteen years ago, when I first started working here, as the newest doctor on staff I wanted all my patients' cooperation so as a bargaining tool I let Mr. Sandoval have a mirror for one night."

"And you feel guilty about it?"

"Not exactly." Tremain went behind his desk and unlocked a bottom drawer out of which came a small locked box. "You must never tell anyone about the contents of this box," he said, "and anyway, even if you did, who'd believe you?" He unlocked the box and pulled out two items: a book and something wrapped in black cloth. "The night I gave him the mirror, security reported hearing a loud scream at around 3:00 a.m. When they arrived at Sandoval's room next to the shattered mirror was this book." He held it up so I could read the title, *Shamanistic Practices of the Navajo*. He handed the second item to me.

"I have no idea how it got into his room or even what it was so I had an anthropologist friend of mine perform some carbon 14 tests on it. As it turns out that thing you are holding does not come from any animal he could identify and even more unbelievable is that it's over 3000 years old. God only knows what damage would occur if this creature were released into our institution. This is why, as long as I am the director, that poor soul in D-18 will never be given a mirror again." I stared in disbelief at the item. It was a fang.

Don't Order That Doll!

The transformation from human Sienna to Sienna, the living, breathing come-to-life doll was underway and Phillip was there to see it all happen, and he had just met her two days before…

He was downing his third Jack and Coke when he first saw her. Utilizing the trick that had worked for him since college, he leaned over her shoulder then grabbed a napkin from the bar counter. He began folding and creasing it over and over. When she finally asked, "What are you making?" Phillip simply looked her directly in the eyes while handing her an origami rose and said, "Anyone can buy you a rose." She smiled and once again he knew the trick worked. He then leaned in closer to smell her perfume.

"I'm guessing Sandalwood."

"And you'd be right," she replied. "I'm Sienna Saunders and you are?"

"Turned on," he replied. Her eyes lit up. "But my friends call me Phillip."

She was immediately attracted to this man and his boldness. The sexual tension in the air was a far cry from what he experienced the night before with his wife…

He'd attempted a few times during the night to have sex but was rebuffed each time. In frustration, he reached over once more, only this time more forcefully. When she grabbed at his arm to push him away, he squeezed her wrist and held it taut against her hip.

He knew he was going too far by forcing himself on her but the overpowering sensation of lust came first before any reason or any feelings of empathy Phillip had for Emma. He clenched his teeth and began breathing through his nostrils intensely like a bull in heat. She gasped in pain, but in his distorted mind it sounded like she moaned with pleasure.

"Stop it!" she cried. Frustrated by his wife's denial of sex, he fumed in the darkness. After all, he reasoned, they were married. She owes this to me. I work hard to give her everything she wants. He finished what he started then rolled over and fell asleep...

And now, here he was in the company of a beautiful, alluring woman who was providing him with needed attention. Earlier in the day, he was taking depositions for a multi-million dollar lawsuit but his mind was elsewhere. As a highly-paid attorney working for a civil litigation firm, Phillip Hardisty's duties were often stressful and today was no exception. It didn't help that he received a call from Emma that made it difficult to concentrate. She decided to spend the night with her sister Lynn after the way he treated her the night before. Phillip was angry at what he felt was his wife's over-reaction and it was affecting his ability to focus.

Whenever there was tension in his marriage, he would smoke a joint then tell Emma he had work to do at the office, but instead he'd usually end up at any number of dive bars in the area. It was at one of his usual watering holes, where he met Sienna. The only difference was this time he didn't have to lie to Emma about where he was.

***

The next day, work was a blur of meetings with partners, phone calls, and more meetings with clients, all with no time in-between. Phillip didn't get home until 7:30 that evening. He had not talked to Emma all day so he was expecting some kind of backlash, instead he found his wife cross-legged on the floor with tears in her eyes, holding one of her Barbara dolls.

He never understood this hobby of hers. Emma had been collecting Barbara dolls since childhood and wasn't going to give it up. Their intoxicating advertising slogan, *Dream Any Dream You Want*, catered to those who were looking to live a fantasy life better than their own, which helped keep customers for a lifetime. With the Barbara line of dolls you could create any life you wanted for yourself (stewardess, banker, biker girl, pop star, the list was endless) and live vicariously through her in the process.

"Stop making this hard on yourself," she said to the doll, chastising it very much like a mother scolding a child. "Quit struggling," she continued. The doll comb had become caught in the hair and she was trying desperately to pull it out. Phillip considered her hobby foolish and the longer he witnessed this scene, the angrier he became. Void of empathy at what he deemed a pathetic sight, he left the house with her sobbing on the floor.

***

The Mosaic bar was the perfect place for a distraction from the unease of his home life. The atmosphere and the lighting were subdued and the bartenders and waitresses minded their own business. He was on his second glass of Cuvee Cathleen Chardonnay when Sienna arrived. She wore a tightly-wrapped silver mesh, low-cut blouse and a short black skirt that made

Phillip's heart race. Within seconds, she caught his gaze and bee-lined her way through the crowd.

"I'm so glad you could come out to play tonight," he said.

"I'm happy you called. By the way, you look pretty good for someone who worked a ten hour day," complimented Sienna.

"Unlike most lawyers I know, I have the ability to shut off that part of my day when I want to—turn it off like a faucet."

"That sounds like quite a talent you have—turning things on and off at will," she replied.

"It is," he said, confidently, "and right now I'm all about turning you on."

He tapped his glass to drink the last few drops of wine but only succeeded in spilling it onto his cheek. Sienna laughed then stroked his cheek with her thumb, slowly bringing the droplets to his lips. She kept it there just long enough for Phillip to nibble on. "I didn't know you were hungry," she responded. "I don't feel like being in a bar tonight," she continued. "Would you like to come over to my place?"

***

Fifty-six minutes after paying the tab, he collapsed face up onto her bed, weakened by the intensity of his desire for Sienna. "Oh my God," he muttered. "That was like a dream—a very steamy and sensual dream—come true. *Whew*!"

"I don't normally spend time with married men," she replied, "but there's something about you I can't resist." With a deep hunger for more, Phillip began kissing her neck when something hanging on the wall caught his eye.

"What's that?" he asked.

"It's a reproduction of a painting known as the wheel of transmigration. Soul transmigration is the essence of the cycle of life itself and not to be taken lightly. It's believed that Buddha himself drew this in the sand to explain the concepts of life, death and rebirth to his disciples."

"You believe your soul leaves your body after death?"

"Your soul is capable of many things, even while you're alive," Sienna replied.

"I've never known anyone like you—the things you say, the way you say them. I'd really like to know more."

"Why?"

"Because I'm fascinated by you. You make life more interesting."

"Well, I've experienced my own form of soul teleportation," Sienna replied, "if that interests you."

"What's that?"

"It's a practice of my soul leaving my body and becoming one with another entity. To start, I put myself into an almost comatose state of relaxation. When I reach that state, in my mind's eye, I become completely removed from all physical boundaries so I can focus every ounce of my energy on communicating with that thing I want to become. Once I've entered the astral plane, I'm so attuned and receptive in this non-physical state-of-mind that I begin to sense vibrations on a different level, like the way a dog can hear a dog whistle but a human can't. I hear the thought vibrations of the thing I want to become."

She continued, "You see, Phillip, the language of thought vibrations is only understandable when in this deep meditative state. When the being's vibrations are receptive, I use my knowledge of spirituality to make the transformation."

"You mean witchcraft?" he interjected. She shot a look at him that said, *Listen and don't talk*, to which he complied.

"Only after I summon help from the other world does the transformation take place. My soul leaves my body and enters the object. I become a mutation, combining my being with everything associated with that object—physical and mental. We become one. I've transported into small animals, fish and even plants. The plants, by the way, are incredibly relaxing—particularly ivies."

"How about inanimate objects?"

"No problem. You simply become it—taking on not only its physical attributes but any and all properties associated with it—that is, if your will is strong enough." Phillip's mind immediately thought about his wife's collection.

"Ever thought about becoming a doll?" he blurted out.

"I've never tried it, but it could be interesting."

"Not you becoming the doll, but rather, the doll becoming you."

"What's on your mind?"

"If it were possible to switch places and instead of you entering the doll, you became everything the doll was, would you do it?"

"Yes, I believe it could be very, very interesting," she replied. They smiled devilishly at each other, intrigued by the possibilities.

***

The next day, Phillip was involved with more depositions and after an hour of questioning, the deponent asked to take a break. Phillip dashed into an empty conference room and called Sienna.

"I have to see you tonight at my place," he said. "I want to see an actual teleportation."

"You just want me again," she replied.

"That's a given. But I really do want to see one."

"Where's the wifey tonight?" she responded, playfully. "Having another sleepover?"

"Yup, back at her sister's. Why don't you come on over around seven? I'll be alone all night."

"I'll be there," she said. "I can't wait to see you."

***

Phillip really enjoyed his time with Sienna. Whenever he wanted to try something sexually deviant with his wife, it was always harshly rejected, but not with Sienna. After a few passionate hours of anything goes fun, Sienna lit her bong, took a big hit then passed it over to Phillip. He took a few hits then showed her the doll he wanted her to become.

Sienna got naked then sat cross-legged on the floor with the doll next to her. "I need complete silence," she said. He lay on the bed, looking down at her as her body was becoming so relaxed she looked like she would collapse any moment. She began to mutter indiscernible phrases that sounded like a mixture of old English intermingled with French, repeating them over and over with the level of intensity increasing with each repeat. Her chanting became sporadic as her breathing became heavier. After about 45 minutes, Phillip drifted off to sleep.

***

He was awakened by what sounded like a gasp for air. The transformation was underway as Sienna felt a tingling sensation coursing through every appendage, inch of skin and strand of hair. It was a meshing of two physical entities with unique properties becoming one. She hadn't shaved her legs that morning and could feel the hairs being pulled inward. Her legs transformed before her eyes into those long and slender gams that every present day model aspires to.

Gone was the three-inch scar below her knee that she got after falling off her bike in 4th grade. Gone were the imperfections in her nails and fingers, now replaced by long slender hands and perfectly manicured nails. All garments and accessories expanded in scale and the limitations of molecular structure and physical boundaries no longer applied to this mutation. Sienna could feel every thread of the doll's clothing, its shoes, and even the play stethoscope (because they were part of what gave that doll her personality) all at once become intertwined with her being. The sight of her changing before his eyes was terrifying to Phillip, while at the same time, amazing to watch.

Sienna looked in the mirror and saw herself now transformed into Nurse Barbara with stethoscope in hand standing before him. With a sultry, sexy voice she asked, "Would you like a sponge bath now, Mr. Hardisty?" Phillip quickly found himself enveloped in this fantasy come true.

***

After transforming back to her own body three hours later, Sienna was physically and mentally drained. In this catatonic state she was barely able to put her clothes back on. Phillip called her name numerous times while she dressed but she simply ignored him then walked out of the bedroom, wandered through the house until reaching the front door and left without saying a word.

***

The next day when Phillip got home from work he saw that Emma was back and he was annoyed. He stormed into the TV room where he heard the barely audible sound of an announcer: *Again, that's item number J7119, this hour's special during our replica antique doll show.* Emma was sitting on the couch, fixated on the screen. Instead of attempting to discuss their problems, he verbally attacked her.

"Damn it. Why the hell can't you clean up this place instead of watching TV?"

"I wasn't feeling well," she replied, numbly, keeping her eyes glued on the show.

"I hope you're not thinking of ordering that kind of doll. It's ugly." Emma remained unfazed. "I'm talking to you," he shouted. "Turn that damn thing off." Her eyes stayed focused on the program, determined not to be pulled into Phillip's pursuit to fight. But he was undeterred. He darted into the room where she kept her dolls and shouted back at her, "Maybe this will get your attention." He grabbed one of the dolls he was least attracted to off one of the display shelves and ripped off its dress just as Emma entered.

"Why are you so cruel?" she cried out.

"Maybe if you gave me the kind of attention you give these stupid dolls, it might not come to this."

Verbal abuse was one thing she had learned to tolerate in their marriage, but something inside her at this moment snapped. She lunged at him, crying out, "It's not stupid! It's who I am. It's what I love." She attempted to strike him but he caught her wrist and pushed her hard into the wall. "Well, that's who I am," he replied.

Emma sank down in despair and cried. He stood over her for a moment then dropped the torn dress and naked doll next to her and left her on the floor weeping for the second time in a week. Emma knew changes had to be made in her life and she would start by moving out for good.

***

Mosaic was more crowded than usual. Phillip and Sienna sat at the corner of the bar, her eyes kissing his while he playfully tugged and caressed her fingertips.

"So, did you enjoy the other night, Nurse Barbara?"

"It was amazing. I felt like something had complete control of me, yet it felt so natural. It even seemed like part of the time I wasn't even there. It's hard to explain."

"The bottom line is—did you enjoy it?" responded Phillip.

"Oh hell yes," she shot back, excitedly. "Can't wait to do it again."

***

Work today was relatively easy. Just a week prior Phillip was buried in depositions and now that the case had settled, he was in a great mood. He couldn't keep his thoughts from drifting toward what pleasures awaited him on those shelves back home. Phillip knew it was wrong to even touch Emma's prized possessions but he didn't care. He had never taken notice of the variety of dolls she had on display but now he was finding himself in a rush to get home so that he could browse the selections at hand. Phillip was now energized with a drive to fulfill every sexual fantasy he could imagine and with Emma now out of the house, he made a point of wrapping his day up by 5:00 so he could have more time to do so with Sienna.

***

"Where'd did you learn this amazing talent of yours," Phillip asked.

"I spent a year in college as an exchange student on the island of Tortola in the British Virgin Islands. A classmate knew of my interest in witchcraft and soul teleportation so one weekend he took me to meet his grandmother who was a practicing Obeah witch. We traveled to her home—a small tin-roofed shack—deep inside the woods. She was a petite woman who hunched over when she walked and she had dark sunken eyes that burned right through you. My friend was her favorite grandson and she took to me right away. As a matter of fact, I ended up spending so much time devoted to learning as much as I could from her, I barely passed my classes. Anyway, that night, we were sitting around a fire drinking Caribe beer when a man and a little girl came wandering out of the woods. She was holding onto a rope that was tied to a goat.

"The man and the grandmother exchanged a few words. Then he went back the way he came, leaving the girl and the goat behind. Moments later, the grandmother spoke some incantations all the while staring directly into the girl's eyes. It was quite a thing to see the girl's eyes change color from brown to a dark red. They then dilated and rolled back while her eyelids fluttered like crazy. It wasn't long before the unthinkable occurred.

"The grandmother shouted, "Speak" and to my fascination the child began bleating while the goat cried like a little girl. It was a complete transference of souls. Moments later, the woman slit the goat's throat from ear to ear. From then on, I was determined to learn everything I could about soul teleportation."

"What happened to the girl?" Phillip asked.

"I'd rather not say," Sienna replied.

***

Emma arrived at the house that night just after 9:00 pm. She had called Phillip multiple times to let him know but he never picked up. All she wanted to do was grab some extra clothes and belongings and leave. The only light she saw came from their back bedroom. Rather than walk in the front door, her curiosity got the better of her and she decided to see if Phillip was alone. Creeping alongside the house, she remembered he always kept the window open this time of year so she was extremely careful about not making a sound. As she got closer, she heard intense moans and peeked inside to see Phillip and a brunette in the midst of *in flagrante delicto*.

Emma was in shock but couldn't stop staring. There was something oddly familiar about what this woman was wearing. She was dressed in a cheerleader outfit and Emma noticed a big letter B on the front of the sweater. She then noticed the pom poms on the bed and gasped in horror. *This whore was dressed like one of her Barbara dolls.* Emma's knees trembled and her heart raced, but she was unable to turn away from this betrayal. She'd suspected Phillip of having affairs but always gave him the benefit of the doubt. When it was over, Emma was sick to her stomach. She was pondering what to do next when something bizarre happened.

The brunette's body began convulsing uncontrollably. Phillip sat up on the bed and watched with interest her spasmodic shaking, which lasted only a minute. Then she fell behind the bed, out of Emma's sight. She then saw Phillip help the woman up who was now completely nude. They embraced for a moment then the woman bent down and picked up something. *How could it be so?* Emma gasped when she saw the woman holding her Barbara Cheerleader. Phillip suddenly turned toward the window to let the blinds down. Emma had retreated to her car just seconds before in a state of complete nausea, throwing up on herself as she sped away.

***

She returned to her sister's apartment that night in tears, ashamed of her life. "This makes absolutely no sense," said Lynn, after hearing Emma's story. "You're suggesting this woman became one of your dolls."

"I know it sounds insane but if you'd seen what I did…there's no other explanation."

"What are you going to do?"

"I don't know," said Emma, "but this evil aberration of nature must be stopped."

***

Two days later, Phillip got a voicemail at work from Emma:

> *I know you've been touching my dolls. I've been going to the house while you're at work to pick up some things and no matter how hard you try not to let it show I can tell they've been moved. I ordered a special edition doll that's worth a lot to me. It just got delivered and in order to keep its value high I'm keeping it in its box. I don't want you under any circumstance to touch it. I can forgive all your past invasions of my privacy and we can go forward from here if you do this one thing.*

There was a defiance in her voice that Phillip had never heard before and he didn't like it. He called Sienna right away to tell her about the special order doll. To this she replied, "I love when someone tells me not to do something. I'll be over tonight." She instructed Phillip to have the door unlocked and the lights out. When she arrived she could barely see Phillip sitting up on the bed. Next to him was a sealed, plain and unmarked box. All the lights in the bedroom were off and the room was pitch black.

"Hand me the box," she said. "Let's make it even more exciting."

"What did you have in mind?"

"Let it be a surprise to both of us," she replied.

This time, it didn't take long before the transformation began to happen. Moments later he felt the warmth of her legs against his as she straddled him. Her soft breathing gently into his ear excited him instantly. "I've got something for you," she whispered. "Are you ready?"

"Yes," he panted but the unexpected pressure of a cold blade pierced his stomach and made him wince in confusion. "What are you doing?" he blurted out.

"Making life more interesting," she replied. He tried pushing her off but with inordinate strength given to her by dark forces, she had no problem keeping him at bay.

And then the stabbings began. "One, two, three," Sienna counted each assault under her breath. "Four" Plorkk! That time she hit bone and it pissed her off as a sharp electric-like pain shot through her hand and wrist. By now, Phillip was beginning to go into shock and was still completely unaware of why Sienna was attacking him. By the hint of moonlight entering the room he noticed a peculiar reaction coming from his lover turned assailant.

He could see she was smiling and he heard her breathing become heavier. He recognized she was getting sexually aroused. In a sick, masochistic way, it almost turned him on to see her like this. Five, six, seven, eight, nine, ten, she stopped counting. When she punctured his lung, Phillip gasped in pain and any strength he had left was now gone.

By the fifteenth stab, she was panting and moaning and stabbing non-stop until finally she climaxed. She regained her composure and took a moment to observe the contortions in

Phillip's face. If it weren't for his yelping and moaning, his expressions, she thought, would look comical. Sphhhlt! Sphhhlt!..stabs 22 and 23 sounded exactly the same to Sienna. She now began a grisly game of trying to repeat the same stabbing sound… Schunk! Shluk! Sshhluck! Schloook!…Nope, she couldn't do it.

At stabbing 28 her hand was so saturated with Phillip's blood it kept sliding off the handle. He began to breathe with short gasps as his lungs filled with blood and she couldn't help but laugh as he looked like a fish out of water. As Phillip began to lose consciousness, Sienna began to lose interest. She decided she wanted to see her handiwork and turned on the nearest side lamp. Phillip saw her and now he understood it all just as she slit his throat.

***

The amount of blood in the room was massive. In his twenty years on the force, Lieutenant Angert had never witnessed a crime scene as vile as the one before him. The medical examiner on site recorded 38 stab wounds on the victim from his chest to his thighs, some of which were made after death and his throat was slit so deeply from ear to ear he was close to decapitation.

Angert looked intensely at the large intestine protruding outside the wound, which was now bubbling over with pancreatic juice. "This sicko really did a number on this guy," he proclaimed. The smell from the body induced an acidic reaction in Angert, causing him to re-taste the sushi and miso soup he had earlier for lunch. Feeling nauseous, he squatted down for a moment and that's when he noticed the box at the foot of the bed.

After wiping away a layer of blood, he was able to read the box label for its contents: *Barbara Doll Special Edition*. Underneath were the words: *Widow Maker—She Loves Men—To*

Death! (Dagger Included). But, try as they might, no weapon was ever found, and because polyvinyl chloride, a thermoplastic polymer used to make dolls, doesn't leave DNA or fingerprints, the murder of Phillip Hardisty was never solved.

Epilogue

She's gorgeous, thought Sam. *I'll just keep buying her drinks and see where this goes.* The woman took another sip of wine and let her shoe casually drop to the floor. In an instant, Sam could feel her toes sliding up his ankle as she playfully tugged at his wedding ring. "Oh, don't worry about that," he said. "We're separated—on our way to divorce." They looked lustfully into each other's eyes until finally she spoke,

"This may sound weird, but I have a doll fetish and there's a particular favorite I'd like to show you. Can we go back to your place?"

"Absolutely," he replied. Sam could care less about dolls but he was curious about her. He paid the tab and wrapping his arm around her waist asked, "What's your name, again?"

"Sienna," the woman replied, "but you can call me Barbara."

Good Night, Sleep Tight

Hayden had been tossing and turning all night and Lori Rae saw this as the perfect opportunity. She got out of bed and returned shortly, handing him a cup of liquid, which he eyed cautiously. "You want to sleep, don't you?" she said, responding to his look. With ten advertorials as well as the copy for two print ads due on Tuesday, Hayden knew he had to get a solid night's sleep. He didn't care much for spending his Saturday at work, but it was a holiday on Monday so that took away some of the sting.

"I'll drink this on one condition," he said.

"What's that?"

"You put Blueberry in the other room so she doesn't disturb my sleep."

"Fine." She picked up the blue tabby, put her in the living room and closed the door.

"Thanks, baby," he said then swallowed the mixture in one gulp.

"You're welcome, baby," she replied. He took comfort in his wife's smile but only had the energy to return a yawn, relieved at the thought that soon he would be knocked out with an eight hour pass to La La land.

***

The effect of the drugs had quickly deteriorated Hayden's ability to comprehend. "Hayden, can you hear me?" Lori Rae called out. "Uh…yeah," was all he could mutter back. She knew it wouldn't be much longer, so she continued: "I've tolerated a lot through the years. I didn't mind your drinking or even your weekend sleepovers with your buddies after those all-night casino binges. Yes, we could've used those thousands you gambled away as the baby is due in four months, but those things I can forgive. Do you remember before we got married me telling you the one thing I cannot?" Hayden was only able to move his lips unintelligibly.

"Did you think I would never find those pictures or those various calls to those sluts? When it comes to your phone security, you aren't the hardest person in the world to figure out, so now it's time for you to pay for your fun while I…" She placed her hand on her protruding stomach…"while we go on vacation. It's only fair. After all, my mother is getting too old to come out to California and I do miss her so." In his lax and sleepy state he thought he heard her say the word "affair" but was too far gone to defend himself. Lori Rae then put on a pair of surgical gloves, walked over to the closet and returned with a small container, which she shook for a moment. She snapped her fingers multiple times just inches from Hayden's head but received no response.

***

Hayden was now dreaming of sharp-toothed lions grabbing and pulling the flesh off carcasses. He stood just inches away and was terrified, and this terror kept him immobile. His feet and legs were like cement and he was unable to move even when the beasts stared at him directly, eyes to eyes. And in his dream his heart pounded ferociously, and the terror rose to nightmarish heights, yet he was still unable to move or awaken.

His leg moved violently once and for a moment this startled Lori Rae. After sharing a bed for six years she knew his habits and that he sometimes twitched a leg or an arm right before awakening from a nightmare. She leaned in closer, so close she could feel his breath on her cheek, all the while her heart raced, thinking her plan would be spoiled if he should wake up.

And what if he did? What then? Her bags were already packed and sitting by the door and her ticket to New York was tucked away in her purse. This trip had already been planned long before she found out about his affairs so this weekend she would be away and it would be the perfect alibi. But after a minute he remained asleep and her confidence returned.

"They say you can get anything you want online," Lori Rae spoke matter-of-factly to the now unconscious Hayden. "Who knew I'd find some nobody in Arizona willing to do anything for money. Let's see…it cost me 1000 dollars for his services, which included a guarantee of discretion, a hundred for the extra ingredient to that slumber potion you just devoured and another 200 for that special couple…horrid little things. I especially appreciated his no paper trail policy…that is, no checks or credit cards…strictly cash. Although I was a bit surprised, but I probably shouldn't be, how easy it was to receive everything in the mail but you know how lax our mail system is these days, what with hours and manpower being cut, our boys and girls in baby blues just don't give it their all like they used to."

"Hayden! Hayden! Are you even listening to me?" She continued, "You know, you can be so rude at times." Then as if on cue, she broke out with a maniacal laugh. "I'm sorry. I couldn't help myself. I was just thinking how sometimes a person can be talking about someone while they're in the same room and that person being talked about will say, "I can hear you. I'm right here." Well, I find it amusing and ironic that you can't even do that." She laughed again for a few moments all the while digging her fingers into their respective palms to the point of making herself bleed.

"Where was I? Oh, yes, just in case you were wondering, there were no searches done from my computer regarding tonight's little drama. It was all done on yours…again, your passwords were too easy…dumbass." She grabbed a book out of her purse and tossed it on the bed next to Hayden. "Don't get me wrong," she continued. "I'm not expecting anyone to question why you suddenly disappeared, not your only remaining relative, dear old dad, nor any of those sluts you were with, not even your work buddies. Because you know what I've noticed through the years? People just don't like you that much. They simply tolerate you."

She looked at herself in the dresser mirror then began a dialogue with an imaginary police officer: *I suspect, officer, he finally left me for one of his younger girlfriends. Check his phone. I'm sure it will tell you all you need to know.* She stopped and admired herself, exclaiming, "I should have been an actress." Then she turned back around to Hayden. "If someone does find you before I return, there won't be an autopsy because I'll play the part of the distraught, pregnant wife so well and I'll insist that it was your wish to be cremated."

She then put their mailbox key on his key chain then glanced again at the mirror and got back into character: *Officer, he always insisted on getting the mail himself. I had no idea he was interested in formicary matters.* "I know what you're thinking," she said to Hayden. "Why go through all this trouble? Well, my dear, it's because, I'm a scorned woman and hell hath no fury like me and also because I fucking can."

"Let's see. What am I missing?" She looked down to see her kitty purring up at her. "Oh, my God, I almost forgot you, my little precious." She set the cat gently into its carrying case then returned to Hayden. "And don't worry about cleaning up while I'm gone. My first order of business when I return will be to get rid of what's left of you…and to call an exterminator. Anyway, I've got a plane to catch and you've got some sleeping to do." She proceeded to pour the entire contents of the container on his face and exclaimed, "Say hello to my little friends."

***

Voracious and curious about the meal before them, the 300 army ants wasted no time in digging their long toothed mandibles deeply into Hayden's cheek. Lori Rae looked on for a few minutes to insure the two deadly Black Bulldog ants were among them. As she observed, Hayden's face twitched slightly. It was the only part of his body moving as she had incapacitated him by slipping in 40 mils of Ketamine, an anesthetic-type drug, along with the sleeping powder. He was quite unable to stop the festival of fangs now drawing his blood in spurts. The red stuff oozed out and this gave Lori Rae much joy and made her smile.

"Well, I guess that's everything," she said, "oh, and I'm afraid you won't be seeing me again after today—as your eyeballs are now being eaten out of their sockets as I speak." She cackled insanely then exclaimed, "Goodnight, sleep tight…well, you know the rest." And with that she picked up her purse, luggage, Blueberry and walked out the door and down the stairs of their condo. Stopping next to the window of their bedroom, she listened for a moment to the faint sound of hundreds of tiny snapping noises that seemed to click in unison to the loud buzzing in her brain. While inside, the morning light seeped in through the blinds with the promise of a new day as Hayden's blood trickled down his face, covering the front of the book entitled, *Raising Ants for Profit.*

Final Audition

"It was April 19th, 2008," began the speaker. "I'll never forget that date because it was the last time I saw my dear friend…"

Jacintha Cross was about to meet a very important theater producer and it gave her a vicarious thrill to be meeting him in such a mysterious way. It was the first time since leaving the small Northern, California town she grew up in and her tragic past that she felt her career might actually go somewhere. As she walked down the hallway, admiring its art deco décor and low lighting, there was something disconcerting about the hotel.

Nearing her destination, a man who appeared quite inebriated, walked unsteadily toward her. He stopped in front of room 613 and attempted to use his card key. After a few unsuccessful tries at unlocking the door he kicked it in frustration. As if in response, there came a resounding angry bang on the door from inside the room, which startled them both. The man stared at the card then at the door number for a moment then realizing his mistake, walked away.

The hallway was now empty and eerily quiet as Jacintha thought back on the day's events that brought her here:

She was performing in a play—a comedy—about a college student sleeping with multiple partners while engaged to be married. The house was only half full and it wasn't until

Jacintha's last appearance onstage that she noticed a man in the second row staring at her. This incredibly handsome admirer, seated in the middle section, was dressed like he was the most important person in the room but was completely fascinated with her.

After the performance, there was a phone call backstage from a man named Ambrose Abernathy who spoke with an uneven cadence in his voice and who kept repeating her name very slowly and deliberately…Jacintha…Jacintha, but there was conviction in his words and he convinced her to meet in his hotel room that night for drinks and to discuss her career.

***

She knocked timidly. The door creaked open slightly, revealing a room of total darkness. "Ambrose?" she called out. No one answered. *Maybe he's testing my impromptu skills as an actress.* Jacintha giggled nervously and entered as the door shut behind her. She stood in the darkness, pondering what to do next. *If I leave now, he may never contact me again and there goes my big break.* When none of the lights worked, Jacintha felt it would be best to wait outside, but as she reached for the door a song began playing from inside the room.

It frightened her at first until she recognized the mellow voice of Gene Austin singing *Tonight You Belong to Me*. This was one of her father's favorites, as he was a huge fan of the early crooners, but there was a peculiarity in the vocals as if the speed of its playing was uneven and it made her feel uneasy.

Suddenly, the lights came on and Jacintha saw the music was coming from a portable wind-up gramophone sitting in the corner. A look around revealed the room to be barren and simple. In fact, there were no modern devices in it at all—no television nor radio or phone, not even a coffee maker. *He must have a reason for all this*, she rationalized again and decided to sit and wait.

Her thoughts drifted to earlier that day when she had told Carlos, the stage manager and her confidante, all about Ambrose. Carlos tried to talk her out of going and she had laughed off his overprotective manner. But just to ease his mind, she promised she would send him a picture she had taken of Ambrose from backstage. During the last scene in the play, the house lights went up. The play was one of those *drop the fourth wall and let the audience be part of the action* kind of plays and it was during that time Jacintha took the picture.

The music jolted her back to the hotel as a sadness now welled up inside her. Hearing this particular song was bitter-sweet because it was the last one her father enjoyed before dying, at least that's what the firemen surmised when they found the remains of an old 78 rpm record melted over the turntable next to his charred body. As she stood up to turn it off, the music stopped.

Jacintha looked around for an air conditioner as the room had suddenly become very cold, but there wasn't one. The lights flickered then went out completely as a perfume odor filled the room and made her gag. *I'll just open the door*, she thought, but the knob didn't turn, as if it were locked from the inside. She banged on it and yelled for help but no one came to her aid. *Duh, I'll just call the front desk*, she scolded herself. But after discovering that her cell phone was dead, Jacintha became scared.

As if on cue, music began playing again, but this time at different speeds: slowing to a snail's pace then speeding up then slowing down again, as if someone or something was taunting her, then stopping completely. Down below, the streets were filled with the usual Saturday night bar hoppers and she tried getting someone's attention by knocking on the window, but not one passer-by stopped to look up. The full moon allowed her to see her cold breath hitting the pane as the temperature in the room had now dropped below thirty. Jacintha began to wonder if she was hallucinating when suddenly she was startled by the touch of a hand on her shoulder. As she turned around, the lights clicked on and the music returned, playing at the correct speed.

Standing before her was her father, robust and smiling. "Dad" exclaimed Jacintha, through her tears. He didn't say a word but simply held his arms out toward her. She happily hugged him, forgetting (at least for the moment) he'd been dead for six years, but life can be cruel as it sometimes portions out happiness and gloom equally and so the joy of seeing him once more was vanquished within moments as his body became hot to the touch and she felt it shrink within her arms. Confused, she looked at him and gasped as the skin on his face began to blister, split apart and then melt off. Suddenly, his eyeballs burst, first the left then the right, splattering watery fluid all over Jacintha's face. The smell of burning flesh now dominated the room and made her feel dizzy. She closed her eyes hoping this would all go away for she knew this was all some sort of evil illusion.

Upon re-opening them, she saw a beautiful, dark-haired young woman dressed to the nines in a pink satin dress and white evening gloves. Panic set in and Jacintha's breathing became labored. She was barely able to utter the words, "Who are you?" The woman simply smiled and said nothing. Then the smile disappeared, replaced with a look of terror, which filled the dark-haired woman's eyes completely. She grabbed her throat in agony as blood squirted through her fingers.

The lights went out again and in this total darkness, Jacintha was so afraid she began to cry. At that moment, she felt the touch of a man's hands on her neck. They were soft and warm and as he began to sing along with the song, tenderly in her ear, "*Tonight, you belong to me…*" she felt comforted. "Ambrose, I'm so glad you're here," Jacintha said. She reached out to put her arms around him but nobody was there, and as the grasp around her neck became tighter and she began to choke she realized he or "it" was not there to comfort her but to claim her.

She desperately seized the knob, which surprisingly turned this time. The door opened and she could see the hallway outside as a young couple holding hands walked by, ignoring her as she tried to get away. A little girl walking behind the couple dropped her stuffed giraffe at the foot of the door and looked up for a moment and it felt as if their eyes locked. Jacintha was hopeful that soon the little girl would call out to her mommy and daddy to help her break free of death's grip but instead she picked up her animal and ran toward her parents, completely unaware of Jacintha's plight.

With only moments left to live, she remembered the hairpin her father gave her on her twenty-first birthday. It was silver with ruby inlays, shaped in her initials, J-C. Tearing it out of her hair she stabbed at his hands repeatedly but to no avail. He was too strong. She heard him whisper, "Out, out, brief candle." She still hoped someone would come to her rescue, but no one did, nor could they because, although outside the room it was the year 2008, inside, she was trapped by an evil force that was manipulating and distorting time for its own selfish needs.

The speaker continued, "Jacintha was found dead outside that same room and to this day no one knows who did it because the killer was never found."

The students stood silently, a bit shell shocked from the tale just told. Carlos knew he had embellished quite a bit but he was in front of a captive audience and couldn't help himself. After all, he was telling a story to answer the question asked by Beth, one of the students, earlier in the tour. He'd been in theater and around actors all his life so Carlos felt obligated, almost driven to tell Beth and the whole class his version of a cautionary tale.

He took a moment to pause, then continued: "So the answer to the question asked earlier by Beth—Is there a shortcut to fame? I'd say there is no substitute for hard work. If you think acting is a means to end and that glamour and glitter are the goals to work for, then you have turned the craft and art of acting into little more than the street where the prostitute flourishes."

"Prostitutes can make a shitload of money," Beth replied. This elicited laughter from her classmates because they all knew her aspirations and wily ways of getting what she wants.

"There's nothing wrong with wanting fame," replied Carlos, "as long as you know that it comes with a price. Take this group of actors, for example." The students noticed the photo Carlos was pointing to that hung on the backstage wall. "Those of you hoping to become an actor should aspire to be as good as Daguerre's Daredevils. This amazing group of daring actors performed plays that dealt with controversy—everything from questioning patriotism to abortion and other social issues that pushed the envelope, not only for their time, but even by today's standards. Led by that handsome man, Daedalus Daguerre, seated in the middle of the photograph, the group was the talk of the theater world throughout the 1920's and thirties, but their popularity ended too soon as a result of their fame.

"In addition to performing successful plays, they did anything they wanted, including throwing wild parties, where sex, drugs and booze flowed freely. Their leader, Daedalus, whose portrayal of Shakespeare's Macbeth was the best I've seen, bar none, would always say, and I quote, *after midnight anything goes*. There were rumors he dabbled in the occult and made everyone, especially the women, dedicate themselves to worshipping him. To prove their devotion they were expected to take part in sadomasochistic rituals. This debauchery, unfortunately, resulted in a number of actresses being murdered at the hands of this obsessive madman. Toward the end, he got so bold he didn't care where he killed. One victim's throat was slit right where we're standing.

"When the police discovered he was behind these murders, Daedalus jumped out a 6th floor window of the Emerald Hotel and crushed his skull on the pavement below. He was a brilliant actor who lost sight of the gift he had." Carlos rubbed his tired eyes. "Sorry, but I'm going to have to cut it short. It's been an exhausting day that's now catching up to me. Thank you all for your attention and I hope you enjoyed the tour."

"It was very informative," replied Mr. Harless, the students' drama teacher. "Okay, class, we need to get back so if you would all thank Mr. Castaneda, we'll be on our way." The class applauded then one by one the students thanked their host, all the while Beth fixated her gaze on the image of Daedalus Daguerre. As they left, Carlos called out, "Come back anytime. The theater loves the curious." Beth turned around to see Castaneda's dark eyes staring directly at her and she felt mesmerized.

***

Once again without an audience, the theater became as quiet as a cemetery at dusk. Carlos grabbed the flask of whiskey he kept hidden in the drawer of the small backstage desk and returned to the row of pictures hanging on the wall. He took a large swig then smiled as he straightened out *Daguerre's Daredevils*. "You sure were a handsome one back then," he said, fixing his gaze on the back row of the picture where a young Hispanic stood, smiling proudly with dimples that radiated. Then he stared at the image of Daedalus long and hard. He took another swig and said, "Our agreement, my friend, I'm sorry to say, is no longer…agreeable to me.

"Being your conduit, so to speak, in this world so you could continue your depraved ways in the afterlife was a thrill in the early days, I must admit, and you certainly kept your part of the bargain. Don't get me wrong, I cherished the hedonistic existence of the eternal youth you gave me. I've experienced more pleasures of the flesh than any one man has a right to, but as the years have gone by, and friends and family got older and died off, it's become less pleasurable and more of a curse. Those few acquaintances I do have continue to ask why I never get older. I feel one day they'll discover the truth that I sold my soul to become no more than a mere understudy to the great Daedalus."

He then pulled a thin, pointy metallic object from his pocket, held it up at the image of Daedalus and continued, "As you said yourself repeatedly on this very stage, *Life's but a walking shadow, a poor player that struts and frets his hour upon the stage and then is heard no more.* All those young and talented actresses didn't deserve what they got. To all of you, I'm sorry." He took one final swig then pulled the straight-razor upward along his arm, severing the radial artery and was heard no more.

***

The drama students were boarded on the bus back to school when suddenly Beth gasped, "Where's my phone?" Without waiting for a response, she jumped up and ran back into the theater, all the while knowing exactly where she left it.

***

Once inside, Beth called out, "Mr. Castaneda, I had a few more questions," but no one answered. "Mr. Castaneda, are you here?" her voice echoed. The theater was dark and quiet. Beth decided to take advantage of this moment alone to walk out on the stage and take some selfies. She took her phone from her purse and looked out toward the empty seats, imagining every one of them filled with her admirers. She posed as if the Paparazzi were begging for more. After snapping twenty pics, she began flipping through them but was startled when she heard whispering. She pointed her phone flashlight toward the seats but saw no one.

Chalking it up to her imagination, Beth continued to look for that one good pic she could post on Facebook. There were shots of her facing the seats and some with her back to them, but the last picture took her by surprise. She saw someone in the theater, sitting in the 2nd row. She zoomed in and a horror filled her completely when she recognized the man from the photo. It was Daedalus Daguerre. Seated next to him was a woman wearing a hairpin shaped in the initials, J-C. Beth leapt off the stage in a panic and ran toward the door, but it was too late. No one heard her scream as the song, *Tonight You Belong to Me* now resounded loudly throughout the theater and the scent of perfume filled her nostrils.

Through A
Wormhole Darkly

October 16, 1944, Der Riese Facility, Germany

The burst of light blinded everyone in the chamber as Private First Class Gunther Bauer emerged from the traversable wormhole. He just returned from a trip fifty years into the future and everyone involved in the (FTR) Future Third Reich Project was eager to hear about it.

1994 had shown him amazing and unusual sights. There were women wearing almost nothing, walking around with tattoos and men with ears and noses pierced like circus freaks... and the sounds...they were everywhere, non-stop, loud sounds and traffic, lots of traffic and in the sky, jets propelled at amazing rates of speed. Bauer was chosen to take part in these experiments because of his electronics background and military assignment as a radio operator and he prided himself on keeping up with the latest in electronics technology but nothing could prepare him for what he saw.

There were people carrying black boxes half the size of a radio transmitter (but with far less dials) that emitted a variety of sounds and music, places that looked like coffee houses filled with all races of people, but no conversations were taking place, instead each person was focused on individual screens attached to typewriter keys, everyone absorbed in typing, typing like secretaries in an office, hardly ever taking their eyes off the screen.

He'd seen the television with its infinite number of programs and even more impressive array of colors, dazzling colors like a vivid dream. One time on leave in Berlin he'd seen the "people's television" being offered at the *Fernsehstuben* (television parlor) but this television of the future was light years ahead in comparison. The television showed him (in a program called a documentary) that the future offered space travel, technological advancements and gadgets of every shape and size he didn't understand, but he was fascinated by it all. As the first soldier to time travel, he was given strict orders to observe and take notes on scientific advances. It was Hitler's purpose with the FTR Project to learn as much as possible so that his scientists could then develop this technology to further advance his power.

Gunther was the perfect Nazi soldier for the job: flawless physical appearance, dedicated whole-heartedly to Hitler and just-plain curious. Others in his unit kidded him about being "too Aryan" because of his extremely blonde hair and white eyebrows, but Gunther was also easy-going and could always laugh at himself. But when he walked out of the wormhole everyone knew something had changed in him. Bauer's eyes were bulging out of their sockets. He was sweating profusely and could not keep his eyes on any one spot, scanning the room constantly, but these were all strictly outward signs. No one but Gunther could hear the shrieking, screeching man's voice that resonated in his brain. He began screaming to this voice no one else could hear: "Shut up! It is infuriating. Stop it! Go away!"

He pointed to the wormhole claiming a demon was nearby then laughed maniacally, but a roomful of lab techs and scientists were ill-equipped to handle what came next. Gunther leapt at the nearest assistant, slamming his teeth with full force on the man's face and bit off a large chunk. He grabbed clumps of the terrified man's hair and was pulling them out by the bloody roots screaming, "Die devil, die" until finally a guard knocked him out with the butt of his rifle.

Some of the staff suggested that the Führer be notified immediately of this unsavory development. Dr. Reinhardt, the program's director, and his assistant Oskar Engle vehemently rallied against informing Hitler, arguing that in order to determine if Gunther's mental state were a fluke or the norm, they would have to obtain a larger sampling group. Initially, the others agreed to this logic and twenty-four other soldiers were sent through the wormhole, one at a time.

With each new subject, Reinhardt adjusted variables (different departure times, giving the subjects various drugs, including ample doses of Pervitin, the methamphetamine drug used by soldiers on the front lines, starving some, over-feeding others) to see if the outcome would change. Unfortunately, each returning soldier displayed similar psychotic episodes soon after emerging from the wormhole, but none were as extreme as poor Gunther's. When Hitler was finally informed of these developments the project was cancelled and each soldier, including Gunther, was taken away, quietly and mostly in strait jackets, to Theresienstadt concentration camp where they were left in their mentally unstable condition to die, unattended.

When the Germans lost the war, Oskar Engle immigrated to the U.S. and changed his name. With the little money he had saved, Oskar began a new life as Oscar Engel, a local fruit vendor. He was never charged for any war crimes so within a few years his scientific curiosity re-emerged along with the rumors that Hitler had survived the war and was living in Argentina and so he continued experimenting with wormholes in his garage, visiting various points himself in the future in anticipation of the day of Hitler's return. On occasion he even paid derelicts who were desperate for money to travel the wormholes, but Oscar was unable to figure out how to eliminate the after-effects of the crippling paranoid psychosis which manifested on the traveler upon their return, nor could he figure out why he was immune to these side-effects. He theorized perhaps it was because he was older than the other subjects, but it remained only a theory.

The Nazis accomplished time travel at the powerful Der Riese facility by accelerating one end of the wormhole with massive electrical charges to a high velocity relative to the other, which resulted in the accelerated wormhole mouth aging less than the stationary one so that when a person walks through it, they come out the accelerated end in the future. With the other mouth being stable you could return through the wormhole out of this mouth soon after you left. Oscar's garage facility was only capable of generating enough electricity to accelerate the mouths of the wormholes he created so that the increments of travel into the future lessened to twenty years instead of fifty. But keeping them stable enough to insure a safe return was more trouble than it was worth so he stopped the experiments by the late '80s all together, even going so far as to dismantle his lab and tear down his garage.

Unfortunately, even after Oscar had taken all these precautions, wormholes would randomly appear then disappear then re-appear approximately 2 hours later for a very short time, only to de-stabilize and disappear for good. Anyone entering them could find themselves 20 years in the future with only a short window to return to their present day. Oscar planted a garden to deter anyone from entering his yard. When that wasn't effective enough, he posted *Keep Off the Grass* and *No Trespassing* signs. No one but Oscar knew of the true danger that awaited trespassers.

June 13, 1996, 7:10 PM

"Go get your brother," said the mother to her oldest son. "He's gone to the 7-11 to buy more of those Teenage Mutant Ninja Turtle cards. He's obsessed with those stupid things."

"Okay, mom," replied Sean, happy to get away from the unappetizing smell of the night's dinner: hamburger mixed with peas and carrots. He was also in no particular hurry to get back home and do his math homework, so he took his time, stopping once to tie his shoe and watch an army of ants devouring a bug on the sidewalk. Then once again to watch a couple of dogs fight.

When he finally turned the corner, he saw his younger brother, Jeffrey, in the middle of being bullied by two other boys. A thin youth, smaller in stature than Jeffrey but with pure anger in his eyes, was clutching his shirt, demanding money. Jeffrey was frozen with fear when Sean appeared out of thin air. Without flinching, he demanded of the thin boy to "let my brother go". This immediately elevated him to hero status in Jeffrey's eyes. The other bully decided it wasn't worth it and mumbled to his friend, "Let's go" to which they both left promptly without a word.

On the way home, Jeffrey was silent for he felt embarrassment at not defending himself. Sean pulled a quarter out of his pocket and tossed it in the air.

"Call it."

"Tails." Despite it being heads, Sean called out, "tails," then said, "Okay, you gotta find me" and this made Jeffrey smile because he enjoyed looking rather than hiding.

***

Back home, the count was on: "One thousand ten, one thousand eleven, one thousand twelve."

Sean had eighteen seconds left. Hiding behind the wheel of his dad's truck was *too easy*, he thought. He then considered the side of the house—*too obvious*. He remembered hiding next to the porch stairs once, but his giggling gave him away.

Jeffrey was up to one thousand twenty-five when a brilliant idea struck Sean—his neighbor's yard would be the perfect spot. There were signs to *Keep off the Grass* but with only five seconds left, he decided to ignore them and dashed across the lawn to the other side of Mr. Engel's house. There, he found a cluster of rosebushes. They were odd in appearance, elongated with a shell-like sphere surrounding them. Sean could hear Jeffrey approaching. He ran toward the bushes and as Jeffrey came around the corner, Sean and the sphere with its strange-looking rosebushes disappeared from sight.

***

Not long after Jeffrey told his parents of Sean's disappearance, the police were at Oscar's door, asking if he'd seen or heard anything. They even searched the perimeter but didn't see what Oscar saw. After a short time, they were satisfied and left. Oscar walked to the side of his house to verify what the police had missed. There it was: the familiar scene he'd witnessed many times before: a gooey residue of exotic matter was dripping from the rose bushes.

***

The Ponces were having trouble coping. Their son had been gone a month now. Friends and family had done their best to console them, but how do you console when you don't know the whys, hows or even the whats?

"We have to face the possibility that we may never see him again," Ruben said to his wife.

"I can't. I don't care how long it's been," replied Elizabeth. "I'll never stop believing he will return to us…somehow, someday." Their nine-year-old was gone and no one—not the police nor friends or family—knew exactly what happened.

Ten Years Later

"It is of utmost importance," the bed-ridden man said, "that you follow my directions to the letter." After a spell of considerable coughing, he continued. "I will be ten years dead and buried when this boy re-appears. You must be there to help him."

"I will."

"Promise me! You must be there! It is my last wish."

"I promise, Father," replied the younger man.

For years, Oscar had seen his neighbors, Ruben and Elizabeth, grieve over the loss of Sean: together, when they held a memorial in his honor, and had even invited Oscar, and separately like the time he saw Ruben on his front porch, weeping while holding the football he used to toss with Sean tightly against his chest. Oscar wanted desperately to tell them both that their son was alive in another time and space, after all he had his own son and understood a parent's pain. And the knowledge he had but could not share gnawed at his conscience every night.

Yes, he'd been responsible for many others going through the wormhole, but these were men, not boys, and they had all chosen to go. The worst unknowable for Oscar was not knowing if Sean had come out the other side mentally stable and this bothered him the most. And now here he was at death's door, wanting to do the right thing...one last shot at redemption.

Oscar handed Frank an envelope and a small box then closed his eyes, and for the first and last time in his life he felt a slight bit of peace for his sins. Moments later, the EKG monitor revealed a flat line. The doctor called the time of death as 4:43 p.m. The cause was brain cancer.

Present Time

Frank looked at his phone. It was 7:49 pm. He wanted to be back on his couch watching game 7 of the NBA finals, wishing this night was already over. But as the Rolling Stones sing, *You Can't Always Get What You Want*. So, he waited, begrudgingly. After all, he wasn't responsible for what happened 20 years ago any more than he was responsible for anything his father did prior to that. Yet, here he was—cleaning up the mess. He took a few more puffs from his cigar then put it out on the sidewalk. It was the longest minute of his life.

7:50 pm

Instead of finding himself behind the bushes, Sean was in front of them. He was trying to figure out how that happened when he noticed someone in the distance standing on the sidewalk directly in front of him. Since it was now dark he couldn't quite make out who it was. Then there was that smell. White Owl cigars—to be exact. It was the same brand his dad smoked so he recognized it immediately. He thought at first this person was his dad and he was in trouble for being out later than usual, but then he recalled his dad never left the house after dark and there was something strange about this man who kept edging his way in closer. Sean reached for his pocket knife—the one his dad gave him last Christmas—but it was gone. *It must have fallen out when he ran to hide.* Under the moonlight, Sean could tell the stranger was his neighbor, Mr. Engel.

Oscar Engel had been living in the neighborhood long before Sean was born, even before his parents moved there. Sean heard growing up how *Oscar the Grouch* chased kids off his lawn—sometimes with a rake or broom in hand. Sean's parents had always warned him to stay away from Oscar because he was old and didn't want to be bothered by kids, but Sean always suspected there were other reasons Oscar was the way he was.

As Sean tried running past, the man reached out and grabbed his arm.

"Wait," he demanded. Sean looked closer at the man's face. He looked like Mr. Engel but something was different. The man's grasp tightened and Sean became truly frightened and struggled to break free. "Don't run away," the man said, his voice slightly softer than before, but Sean learned in school what to do when a stranger grabs you. He allowed his body to become dead weight, which broke the man's grasp. This quick move allowed Sean to scramble to his feet and run home. Upon reaching his front yard, he turned around to see if the man was following him, but he was gone. The front door was locked so he rang the bell. As soon as it opened, he darted inside.

"Excuse me. Can I help you?" said a woman Sean didn't recognize. He was surprised a stranger was opening the door and not his mom. As he tried to recall which of his mom's friends she was, a man he'd never seen before walked out of his parent's bedroom.

"Where's my mom and dad?" he asked the woman.

"I don't know," she replied, "Do you live around here?" Sean didn't respond but instead continued looking for his parents. No one was in the kitchen. He walked into the den and still no one. He banged on the bathroom door—no response. Something—everything was wrong. The color of the kitchen was different. The sofa was leather not cloth and there were different pictures on the walls. The TV was also different, much flatter and larger.

Panic set in as he called out, "Mom, Dad," repeatedly with no response. He opened his bedroom door and saw an older boy sitting on a bed different from his. Sean sat on the floor and examined the room thoroughly with his eyes and the more he saw, the more he felt like breaking down and crying because none of this made sense. It was his room alright but nothing in it was his.

"Robert, do you know who this is?" the woman asked.

"My name is Sean," replied Sean to no one particular.

"Well, Sean, this is our son, Robert."

"Hey," Robert replied. Sean continued looking around the room.

"Sean thinks he used to live here," said the mother.

"Not used to. I do," replied Sean, angrily.

"Robert, Why don't you and Sean hang out for a little bit while your dad and I get this straightened out."

"Ohh-kay," replied Robert.

"Don't worry. We'll be right out here making a few phone calls." Sean noticed the grey object in Robert's lap.

"Wanna play?" Robert asked.

"What is that?" replied Sean.

"A PlayStation."

"What's a PlayStation?"

"It's a videogame controller." Sean sat in amazement as Robert played Final Fantasy on his PS3. It temporarily took away the confusion and pain of not knowing where he was or how he got there. Within a few minutes, though, the spell was broken when Robert asked, "How can you live here when you can see this is my room?" The sudden return to reality angered Sean.

"I live here," he insisted, again.

"Maybe you're lost and your house looks just like ours from the outside," replied Robert.

"No. I was playing hide and seek with my brother and I ran next door to Oscar the Grouch's yard and I tried to hide in some rosebushes and then I came over here."

"Who's yard?" Robert asked with a smirk on his face.

"Mr. Engel's house next door. We call him Oscar the Grouch because he hates when kids get on his lawn."

"A couple lives on that side and on the other side is an old woman, Mrs. Fernandez. There's no one named Oscar," said Robert. "What are your parent's names? Maybe my mom and dad know them."

"Ruben and Elizabeth Ponce," he replied. Robert noticed a sadness in Sean's face as he spoke and he wondered how he'd react if this were happening to him.

"Want to play Final Fantasy while you wait?" Sean shrugged his shoulders. Robert continued, "I'm sure my parents will find out where you live." Sean's despondency turned hopeful as he suddenly walked over to a trashcan in the corner.

"Are you gonna throw up? Do you feel sick?" Robert asked. Sean looked up at him with renewed certainty.

"I burned the floor where the trashcan is." Robert knelt down. "It's under the carpet," he insisted. "On New Year's Eve, my friend, Alex, dared me to light five sparklers at the same time but I dropped them. It made a big burn spot right there." Robert was now intrigued. He grabbed the carpet, trying to pull it up but was interrupted when his parents entered the room with a policeman.

"Sean, this officer is going to help you," said the woman.

"Don't worry, Sean," said the policeman. "We'll get you home all right. I just have to ask you a few questions."

"Okay, sir," Sean replied, "but I need to use the restroom first."

A minute later behind the locked door, he climbed on top of the toilet, popped out the window screen, squeezed through the window, and sprinted down the alley and around the corner.

9:40 pm

Sean knew that if he stuck around, the police might take him away. All he wanted to do was go back home. Something told him Oscar's yard was where all this weirdness began and that he must get back there, but with the police still around he decided for the time being he needed to hide. He ran down the street to the corner of Serling and Bierce—two street signs that looked exactly the same as they did when he and Jeffrey passed them on their way back from the store. That walk home now seemed like an eternity ago.

In the distance, he saw a McDonald's restaurant that wasn't there before, and despite all he'd been through tonight, Sean was still aware of his most basic need. As he searched his pockets for loose change once again he was confronted by the strange man.

"Hello, Sean," he began. "My name is Frank Engel. I believe you know my father, Oscar Engel." *Now it made sense why this man looks so much like his neighbor.* He continued, "You trespassed on my father's yard but when you went home tonight things weren't the same. That's because they're not." Sean listened intently as Frank continued. "I don't mean to frighten you, but you've gone through a wormhole, a time portal, that's transported you twenty years into the future. Today is June 13, 2016. As I believe you've already found out, your parents no longer live in the house you grew up in—the one you've lived in all your life. That life—the life you once knew is gone. Everyone you've ever known—all your friends and family are 20 years older."

Sean knew something was wrong but nothing could prepare him for what Frank was saying. He knew a little about wormholes from science class and theories about how they are all around us but he was still very much a child and couldn't believe what he was hearing.

"You're lying," he said to Frank.

"I wish I was." He pulled out his Android. "Do you know what this is?"

"No."

"That's because this kind of technology wasn't around twenty years ago. Give me a subject you like—anything." Sean was dumbfounded and could only think of his brother's obsession. Barely audible, he whispered, "Teenage Mutant Ninja Turtles."

"Okay, watch this." Frank opened YouTube and found a video of the Turtles which he started playing. "This phone not only plays videos, it plays music, it's my alarm clock, it tells me the weather, the news…I wish we had these twenty years ago." Sean's eyes widened in amazement at this wonderful invention. To be able to carry around a box that played cartoons so small it could fit in your pocket was something he could never have imagined would be possible. The realization that Frank wasn't lying began to sink in and he was overwhelmed with emotion.

"Can you call my parents on that?"

"Sean, I don't think that's a good idea."

"You said it was a phone. I want to talk to my mom and dad." Frank gave a heavy sigh then asked, "What's the number?" For the first time since this whole nightmare began, Sean was hopeful. *They have to answer*, he thought. *Even if they did move, there's no way they'd change the number.* When the recording, *We're sorry, you have reached a number that has been disconnected or is no longer in service*, played it might as well have said, *Sean you no longer exist*. He stood stunned for a moment, unable to find the words.

"No, this is not…this is…no!" Sean could no longer see Frank clearly as the tears welled up in his eyes.

"Where are my parents?" he cried.

"They're somewhere else."

"Where? What's happening?"

"I know it's hard to understand, but you must trust me because I don't have time to explain everything," replied Frank. "The only way you're going to get back to them is if you go back to the rose bushes at my father's house before it's too late." Sean refused to hear anymore. He had to get away from this madness. He ran across the street toward the McDonald's.

9:45 PM

Robert slipped back into his room and locked the door, wondering why Sean left so abruptly. The police had already left to search the neighborhood, so he grabbed the pocket knife he'd recently found in his yard and tore away as best he could a section of the carpet where the trashcan had been. It didn't take long before he noticed a burned spot on the wooden floor underneath. *Whoa*, was all he could say to himself.

***

Approaching the front of the restaurant, Sean wondered if the fifty-three cents he had on him could even buy anything on the menu. All he knew right now was hunger and tiredness. With Frank in the distance watching him, Sean wasn't sure what to do. A voice out of nowhere called out, "No man is an island." Sean looked around and saw a man in dirty, tattered clothes standing by the entrance. He was holding a sign which read, *Wisdom for Spare Change.*

"How's it going?" the man called out to Sean.

"Terrible," Sean replied.

"I'm Sebastian, Sebastian Soledad but my friends call me Seba. I've always thought if there was one thing I was blessed with…it's my name…Sebastian Soledad. It rolls off the tongue so smoothly, I think. I truly believe a name generates a certain kind of energy in a person or a thing. A sloth, for example, can't help but be slow and lazy. It's all in the name; whereas, a lion exudes magnificence; however, Shakespeare did write, "A rose by any other name would smell as sweet" so I suppose the sloth would still be slothy, whatever it was called.

Be that as it may, I've always thought of myself as one cool cucumber because my name sounds cool. When everyone else around me is losing it, I keep it together. I might beg on the streets for my next meal, my friend, but I'll always have that."

"I'm Sean."

"Nice to meet you, Sean. That's a nice name, too…short, sweet and to the point."

Sebastian could see Sean was distracted as he looked out in the distance at Frank.

"Is that dude bothering you?" he asked, sincerely. Sean simply put his head down in sadness. "Rough day, huh?" He tapped on his beat-up, cardboard sign. "See what this says?… Wisdom for spare change. What I didn't tell you is for this hour only I'm running a special…free advice, even if you don't ask for it." Sean found this slightly amusing and smiled. "Let's be honest," he continued. "You don't know me from Adam, but I do know the streets and I can spot someone out of place a mile away. I can tell you don't belong out here wandering around this late at night. Am I right?"

Sean agreed.

"So, if someone out there (he motioned to Frank) can help you get on home, where you belong, you should take their help. Like I said before, no man's an island."

There was something majestic, true and honest in these words and Sean was impressed by the quickness in which Sebastian summed up his dilemma. It was epiphanous and provided clarity in this recent fog.

"Hold on. I've got one more." Rummaging through his pants pocket, Sebastian found a thin strip of paper, formerly the tenant of a fortune cookie, and read, *It's better to have a hen tomorrow than an egg today.* "I have to disagree with that one. An egg sounds pretty delicious to me right now." He reached into his pocket again and read another strip: *You will conquer all obstacles.* "Bingo! That's the one for you."

He then handed Sean a Walking Liberty half dollar. "Normally, I'm the one in need of money," Sebastian said, "but this coin isn't just a coin. It was given to me a couple of years ago by a little boy about your age. His grandfather kept it during the depression and told him to hold on to it for luck until he found someone who needed it more. Truth be told, I've done some terrible things in my life, some I wish I could take back and some I don't regret but the one thing I've learned is I would never wish the kind of desperation I've had on anyone else. That one act of kindness from that boy gave me strength, almost as if his good nature rubbed off so I guess I'm passing it on to you now." Sean stared at the coin's image. "Miss Liberty's supposed to be a symbol of hope and I know we can all use that."

"Thanks." Sean put it in his pocket. Suddenly, a police car pulled into the parking lot, startling them both. Sebastian could see the fright in Sean's eyes. He walked over to two women that were leaving the restaurant and began bombarding them both with requests for money, loud enough for the policeman to approach him. It was the same policeman that was at Sean's house before. Sean saw what Sebastian was doing and seized the moment to run away, undetected.

He crossed the street and walked over to Frank. In the distance, he could see Sebastian being handcuffed and put into the police car. As they walked away, they heard Sebastian shout out, "Three hots and a cot, baby... Whoo Hoo!"

***

Despite being only twelve, Robert was an old soul who constantly yearned for truth. He deduced that finding out about the people in Sean's life might help solve how he got here. He would start with Oscar. After Googling Oscar Engel's name and finding the variant Oskar Engle, Robert found the Wikipedia listing of Franz Oskar Engle, born 1919 in Munich, Germany and concluded they were one in the same.

Oskar was a *wunderkind* who by the age of 17 had earned his doctorate in quantum physics at Heidelberg University. By 18 he was lured by the passion of Hitler's speeches into joining the Nazi Party. In 1942, he'd attained the rank of *Unterscharführer* in the SS and was assigned to a special unit in Der Riese facility near the Czech border. While there, he worked as a security guard where top secret experiments in anti-gravity propulsion were being conducted. These experiments were known as *Die Glocke* (the bell) experiments.

What Robert's research didn't uncover was that in addition to the anti-gravity experiments there were other tests taking place in Der Riese facility. Hitler's scientists had found a way to open traversable wormholes using exotic matter. Because of his advanced knowledge of physics, Oskar was allowed to assist in experiments with Dr. Reinhardt. Together they worked on harnessing the power of artificial negative mass, which helped to control the wormholes.

***

Within an hour, Robert had familiarized himself (as best he could) with Sean's life. He even Googled Ruben and Elizabeth Ponce and found a YouTube video from 1996. The poor quality video began with a newscast:

> *Good evening. Our top story today is about the disappearance of a nine-year-old boy by the name of Sean Ponce. Sean has been missing from his parent's home since around 8 p.m. last night. News Reporter Lucinda Bell is on the scene now with the latest.*

The video continued with an interview of Sean's parents. They were begging the public for information related to the whereabouts of their son, even going so far as to post a reward.

***

Robert's curiosity continued to be fed with other related videos. He learned Ruben Ponce had been killed in a car accident on his way home from following up on a clue from a witness who swore they saw Sean in a mall fifty miles away.

Robert also learned within three months the search had dissipated to just a few family members still following up on every lead. But it was the last video that really jarred him. It

was titled *Brother of Missing Boy Shoots and Kills Eight People.*
Jeffrey had become increasingly despondent after Sean's disappearance and even more so after the death of their father to the
point of becoming a loner.

This last video was dated twelve years to the date of Sean's
disappearance and showed Jeffrey walking into the student
lounge of his community college with a handgun and killing
eight students before turning the gun on himself. Follow-up
newscasts had psychiatrists explaining Jeffrey's state of mind and
that he'd even left a note explaining how unfair life was since the
loss of his brother and father. It was a horrific turn of events that
made Robert physically ill, but it also made him all the more
determined to find Sean, and now he knew exactly where to look.

***

Frank and Sean had been careful to insure no one was around
before attempting to enter the wormhole. All the cops had left
so now was the time. Frank felt the best way for Sean to cope
with what he'd seen and heard was to tell himself it was all just
a bad dream and when he returned to his own time it would
be like it never happened. When they arrived at the bushes, the
wormhole was already there but Frank knew right away by its
fragmenting appearance that it was unstable.

This nightmare of Sean's just got worse and he became
frightened at the prospect of going through the wormhole. As
he stood there, thoughts raced around his brain, crashing into
each other like cars in a demolition derby: Would he really
return to his own time? Would his parents be there like before?
If he stayed here, at least he could search for them. What if the
thing closed up? Would he be stuck in some other time forever?
He began breathing heavily and that's when he saw Robert.

"Who are you?" Frank asked.

"Robert. I live next door and I know why Sean is here."

"Is this true?" Frank asked Sean.

"He lives in my house now…in my room. He knows."

"No, No, No…this is too much," replied Frank. "It's dangerous for anyone else to know. It could change everything. You need to leave now. This is none of your business."

"I have to tell Sean about his future," replied Robert. "There are some things he must know."

"No! Absolutely not," replied Frank. "It could change everything."

***

Two hours had passed since Sean emerged from the wormhole and Frank knew Sean's window to return was closing fast. He opened the box he'd been carrying with him, the one his father gave him on his deathbed, and turned on a small apparatus contained within it. Using the experiments of Dutch physicist Hendrick B.G. Casimir as a jumping off point, Oscar had developed his own negative mass inducer. This contraption allowed Frank to balance the energy in the wormhole, thus stabilizing it. He approached the rosebushes and focused his attention between them and the box. Robert saw this as his opportunity for he could no longer keep quiet. He got on his phone to show Sean the YouTube video of his brother's rampage.

"This is what happens after you disappeared," said Robert. "I'd want to know about my future if I was given the chance." Sean stared at the grainy images of the news reports, trying to make sense of them. In a span of ten minutes, he learned of his father's death and his brother's rampage and suicide. His psyche was exhausted at being pulled in every direction at once and he became truly scared of the unknown.

"I can't go in there," he cried. "Look at it. I'll die if I do."

"I know this is the craziest thing that will ever happen to you and probably to me as well," replied Robert, "but just think what you could change if you go back. Your brother and father don't have to die. All these things happened because you went missing but none of it can be changed now if you stay here."

***

Frank had been listening to Robert but was too focused on stabilizing the wormhole to intercede. He could only keep the wormhole open for another minute before it collapsed for good. "If you are to go, it must be now," he shouted. Sean thought of his family and what they meant to him. He decided he had to do what he could to save them and ran into the wormhole, hoping to come out the other side as before, but instead his body became paralyzed in mid-step.

He felt the sensation of running but without movement as if he were suspended in the air by wires. Then all at once his body became fractured like pieces in a puzzle. He could see his legs dangling above him and his hands floated away, detached. He let out a gasp which created waves of air around him like a stone thrown in a pond and his skin began to melt off before his eyes.

Frank quickly recognized the distortion in space/time and knew there was a way to fix it. There was one drawback to this. He'd have to enter the wormhole himself. With no time to waste, he entered and immediately amped up the negative mass inducer, allowing one last blast to stabilize the wormhole enough for Sean to get through. As soon as it stabilized, Sean's body returned to normal and he was able to continue running. All at once, there was a great light emanating from its center. Robert closed his eyes and upon opening them, saw they were gone and the sphere was no more.

June 13, 1996 10:25 PM

Sean emerged in front of the rose bushes, just like before. He glanced around in time to see Frank and the wormhole disappear. Immediately, he ran past the front of Oscar's house. The tears were hard to keep back as he realized he was home. In his excitement to be back, he didn't notice Oscar peering at him through the blinds as he walked past the front of his house back to his own.

***

Sean never told anyone what had happened. When his parents would ask where he was for those two and a half hours, he'd always reply, "I don't want to talk about it." Returning to his original life had destroyed the alternative timeline created by his entering the wormhole but his reticence to speak about it, even to Jeffrey, would cause a brokenness in the family that never healed. Whenever Jeffrey tried to ask about the night they played hide and seek and Sean disappeared, he would get angry and say, "Nothing happened. Leave me alone."

Every morning Sean awoke he would immediately see if he was still in his own room, in his own bed with his own things. His psyche became a playground for the fears lingering in his sub-conscious: *Would his parents be there every morning when he walked out of his bedroom? Were things really as they used to be?* And he lived like this day-to-day. The future became something to be feared and not anticipated, but he returned to his life as a child as best he could for there was nothing else he could do.

The universe did what it had to do to put things right: the first was that Sean's father (who was never really health conscious to begin with) died at the age of 44 of heart thrombosis. As for Jeffrey, he only lived to the age of 18 and was the victim of an unfortunate accident at his college in which a furnace had exploded in his dorm, killing himself and eight others who were celebrating end of semester finals.

Sean's mother was so distraught by the loss of her husband and son in such a short time, she decided to sell the house and move away. The real estate agent was a good friend and provided her with some small comfort assuring the house was in good hands with the new owners, a young, vibrant couple just starting out with a little baby named Robert. It wasn't until Sean got married and had a child of his own that he felt he was finally home again.

One day, years later, he was walking through the park with his 3-year-old daughter, Elizabeth, when a homeless man called out, "Spare change?" Seeing the occasional derelict in the park was nothing new but there was something different about this one. He knew this man, but how?

"Spare change?" the man asked again.

"Of course," replied Sean. As he handed him a five, Sean realized he was looking into the eyes of Sebastian. Even though it was still years before Sean had actually met him he looked much older. Gone was the ebullience and gusto from before and his eyes revealed a state of weariness and abundant pain. The shock of seeing Sebastian as he now was hit Sean hard and he knew there was no point in revealing himself. He had no way of proving they'd met (the Walking Liberty half dollar was no longer in his possession as the timeline in which it was given no longer existed). The man winced once as if poked with a stick, then said:

"They're coming."

"Who's coming," Sean asked.

"The demons." He looked out in the distance and gasped, "They're here!"

He grabbed at Sean's hand, clutching his jacket. "Help me get away!" His eyes were full of desperation, revealing a truly lost soul. He pulled a rose from his pocket and held it up for Sean to see. It was lacking most of its petals and was covered in some type of gooey residue. "Help me!"

Sean grabbed his daughter's hand and proceeded to walk away quickly. Elizabeth broke free and ran toward a nearby rosebush despite Sean's shouts of, "Elizabeth, Get back here, now!" She wriggled underneath, reaching for something as Sean looked on horrified. "Got it!" she shouted then ran back to Sebastian, ignoring Sean all the while.

"You need a new flower," she exclaimed. Sebastian took the fresh rose from her small hand, carefully, so as not to lose any of the petals. He put it up to his nose and said, "Smells sweet" then he looked at her. She smiled in innocence and he smiled back and for that moment there was no time or space, nothing corruptible, and there were no demons, merely happiness.

A Hand Is a Terrible Thing to Waste

Instinctively, Nestor knew it was wrong but he didn't care. Brash decisions made by seventh graders trying to impress girls very rarely turn out right, but Angela Martinique wasn't your ordinary preteen sweat pea. With straight, dark hair that flowed down her back like silk and heavenly dark brown eyes, she was the most beautiful girl he'd ever seen and just to be in her company gave him sweaty palms.

"Let's go, Angela," pleaded Norma, her friend. "This is so boring!" She rolled her eyes to emphasize her point.

"Please, just a little longer," Nestor insisted. He knew after countless hours of watching the trains that one would be by shortly. He also knew they slowed to a snail's pace at this spot, just across the street from Fred's Fish Fry, and he would have but one shot to impress her. Within moments a train's rumbling was heard. His heart was racing, not because he was scared but because Angela replied to her friend, "Wait, I want to see what he's gonna do."

Nestor had done it once before (when no one was around) and now lifted by Angela's words of curiosity was confident he'd succeed. His best friend, Gonzalo (between the two of them always the voice of reason) tried once more to stop him. "This is stupid!" is all he could think of to say at this late juncture, and it was late, for the moment of truth was upon them. Nestor ran alongside the train with the intention of climbing aboard. Its engine had just passed them and as it lumbered onward, he grabbed onto the open door handle with his left hand and grasped the inside platform of the car with his right and was about to jump onboard, when something caught his stride.

Perhaps it was a rock that the train itself had launched toward him, trying to warn the boy not to proceed with his plan or perhaps it was fate itself chucking its will in his direction. Either way, it was game over. He slipped and fell forward, throwing his hands outward to catch the fall. His body landed with a thud immediately followed by a swishing sound. Laying bruised and battered next to the tracks, he felt a warm sensation coming from his left hand. There was blood seeping out where his hand should be but wasn't.

As the train rattled away, moving forward without a care, unaware of the casualty it left behind, Nestor saw the other children running toward him, and then he saw *it* on the tracks beside him, no longer part of him. At that moment he felt dizzy but he would later swear he saw its fingers still curled and squeezing in unison as if still trying to hold onto the train, trying to hold onto those precious seconds he had of Angela's attention. There was no doubt he had her full attention now. She was screaming the shrillest and most horrifying scream he'd ever heard. His eyes suddenly felt extremely heavy and then everything went dark.

***

For the first few days in the hospital, Nestor had nothing to do but think about the accident. No matter how hard he tried, he couldn't get over the feeling that he was no longer the same. From now on, he would have to learn how to do everything right-handed. Simple tasks would take twice as long as before. As the days passed, he pondered what went wrong, what he could have done differently, and what he'll do differently in the future, and through all this contemplation he came to the conclusion he would keep the severed hand.

Maybe it was because he was angry at God and felt he was dealt a bad hand, so to speak, or maybe he wasn't ready to let it go. Either way, he presented the idea to his mother and justified his decision by saying gallstone patients get to keep their stones, dental patients get to keep their teeth and even new mothers can keep their placentas, so Why not his hand? After all, it was his favorite.

"Why would he want it, Mrs. Galindo?" asked the officiating doctor who was extremely curious to hear her answer. "You do know there is no possibility of it ever becoming attached again."

"Why not? It's his," she replied, summing up Nestor's arguments succinctly. This reply seemed to hit a nerve. Normally, hospitals are required to dispose of detached limbs but a few years back the doctor had lost some toes during a stint in Southern Mexico. He was working for a non-profit organization called *Manos Que Ayudan* (Helping Hands) that provided poor countries with medical aid. His two smallest toes on his right foot were forever gone after he inadvertently stepped on an alligator trap, so he was not without a sympathetic ear (having had first-hand experience) regarding the boy's unexpected, life-changing event.

So life went on and after a month of hospitalization and counseling that was supposed to provide insight on how to adapt to being one-handed in a two-handed world but only succeeded in annoying Nestor, he returned home. His hand, which his mother had taken from the hospital without incident, was waiting patiently at home for his return. The doctor was kind enough to provide a jar of Ringer's solution to keep the hand in. As far as the railroad company was concerned, it neither cared nor worried about Nestor's loss since all fault regarding the accident lie with the boy—hands down.

Being of below average looks and a bit pudgy, Nestor didn't get much attention in school, but when he did return he received somewhat of a hero's welcome from his classmates. It wasn't long before the whole school knew him as "that guy with one hand" and his popularity soared. Everyone wanted to hear what had happened. He didn't even mind the cruel and mean-spirited remarks (at least once-a-day someone would hold out their hand and shout, "Wanna shake on it?"). All the while, Nestor kept hoping he would run into Angela. He didn't know what he would say just that he wanted to see her. She was so shook up about the incident, she changed her schedule to make sure she didn't have any classes with Nestor and he never saw her again.

Fame is fleeting and it wasn't long…weeks, in fact, before his popularity diminished back to its non-existent state and when you're twelve, being popular is everything. Nestor wasn't too keen on going back to being invisible again. He decided to do something about it—something that made sense to his young and impressionable mind. To keep the momentum of popularity going, he would create a Facebook page for his hand.

He gave it as interesting a profile as he could imagine. It included the hand's favorite books: *Catcher in the Rye* and *To Kill a Mockingbird*, television shows (it really loved *Breaking Bad and Bates Motel*) and even films: *Cool Hand Luke* and *The Hand That Rocks the Cradle*. When the time came to create its profile pic he tried various ways to enhance the hand's jar.

First, he tied a black ribbon around it but that was too somber. Then, he tried a light-hearted approach by slapping some psychedelic temporary tattoos on the jar—a leftover prize from a box of Cracker Jacks. That seemed too girlish. He finally settled on tying a red bandana around the wrist stump because he felt it deserved the reputation of a bad-ass, and after showing the pic to Gonzalo, they both agreed the red bandana really did make the hand's grey fingernails pop.

Next, he placed the jar on top of his dresser next to the picture of his Confirmation: his mother smiling proudly on his left and to his right stood Father Joe, his left hand neatly placed on the boy's shoulder. His own father, absent from his life for many years before, was not in the picture. He turned the jar around trying to capture the sunlight through his bedroom window until it burst magically through the hand's fingers just right—a handsome shot, indeed.

By month's end, Lefty, as he had named it, had 450 friends, with requests coming in daily. This was 430 more than Nestor had and that included family. The powers that be at Facebook saw no harm in Lefty's page and because it was not vulgar or obscene (just a bit weird) it was allowed to remain open. Its views tended to be liberal, of course, being a lefty and it was getting "likes" for everything it said or posted. Lefty spread its share of likes for everyone and everything from birthdays to bar mitzvahs. It smiley-faced newborn babies and sad-faced announced deaths.

The boy relished the attention Lefty received which enhanced (if only vicariously) his online social life because it was after all, he, as the voice of Lefty, who responded to anyone wanting to know all about the hand's life. And the questions were as varied as the people asking them: How often do you have to change your water? How's your love life? Ever been a model? Who's your favorite Beatle? What are your thoughts on the U.S. policy on global warming? Are you goth or gangster? And the questions and comments did not let up.

He began taking more pics to enhance its page. It started with simple selfies of Lefty in bed, relaxing, Lefty chilling to music and Lefty watching TV. But as its popularity grew, Nestor felt he had to give Lefty more of a life because he knew the more pics he posted, the more likes he'd get. So, he took Lefty out of his jar once in a while, gave him a quick wash to remove some of the smell, threw him in his backpack and off they'd go: to the park, bike riding, and errands to the store (although he knew better than to frivolously display it while in the meat section—that would be in bad taste).

One time Nestor and Gonzalo were at the zoo next to the monkey cages. He was showing Lefty to a group of teens when a curious gorilla with extraordinarily long arms reached out and tried to pull it away. It would have succeeded if Nestor's right hand and arm hadn't become so strong for now it was doing the work of two. The pinnacle of second-hand recognition for Nestor came when Angela sent Lefty a friend request and commented, "You're so cute!!" In return, Nestor sent her a friend request from his own Facebook page but she never responded.

At its peak with 1,250 friends, the boy had grown weary of keeping up with Lefty's popularity. He found himself spending more time online than doing homework, watching TV or just hanging out. Besides, the hands of time spare no one or no thing from the ravages of age, and Lefty began showing signs of withering and decomposing at a somewhat rapid pace despite it being preserved nicely in the jar for a while. Also, the people that find these things worth their time were now more interested in a chicken with three heads, born in Brownsville, Texas, by the name of Mrs. Feather Bottom that had become the latest social media sensation.

Nestor was now nearing fourteen and ready to get on with his life. "I'm sorry," he said to Lefty, one day after school, "but I'm closing down your Facebook page. It's just taking too much of my time." This upset the hand and it turned slightly in its jar so that its dried palm with fingers, rigid and pointing straight to the sky, faced Nestor as if to say, "Talk to the hand!" Then it floated around defiantly (or so it seemed) so that its back faced the boy and he felt disrespected...by his own hand. That kind of contempt sealed the deal for Nestor and he deleted all the pictures (except for the profile pic—he was still proud of that one) and as simple as that Nestor said goodbye to his fifteen minutes of fame.

As he grew older, occasionally out of curiosity, nothing more, he would log onto the hand's page to see if there was anything of real interest. The last significant attention Lefty received was from a group of enthusiasts called *Handy Hands*. They wanted to see Lefty's page restored to its former glory and posted inane comments such as, *All we are saying, is give hand a chance!* But their own Facebook page logo too closely resembled a very powerful charity's logo and they were soon slapped with a cease and desist letter. This put an end to what remained of Lefty's devotees. After that, the only interest in Lefty was an occasional request to play Candy Crush.

By the time he was sixteen, Nestor had all but forgotten about Lefty. A while back he'd placed the jar in the far corner of his closet because the hand dried up and began to smell. On his seventeenth birthday his mother had given him an artificial hand with Bluetooth capability, so now it was time to say goodbye.

One Saturday evening he made a pilgrimage with the jar back to the tracks where it all happened—where he lost more than just an extremity. It seemed so long ago and when Nestor arrived he couldn't remember the exact spot. Fred's Fish Fry had gone out of business years before when a patron claimed to have found a finger in her fries, so there was no other point of reference. Nestor walked up and down the tracks, finally settling on an area where a patch of weeds grew wildly and standing alone within it was a single purple lilac. He clawed at the dirt next to the lilac just deep enough to put Lefty into the ground. Those attending the funeral included a rusted soda can, a few cigarette butts, a smashed penny and the breeze.

He reminisced about Jr. High school and reflected on those things that seemed important then but were now a fading memory and a sadness overtook him. He didn't truly understand why but it was enough to make his eyes water. He waited for the train, an appropriate symbol of closure, he thought, but it never came and anyway, he was late for a date with Angela. No, this was not the same Angela from before. He would have given his left hand for just one date with her (which he did). She had transferred to a different high school and it was rumored gotten pregnant twice already and had two abortions.

Tonight's date was with another Angela…Angela Esperanza. She wasn't nearly as pretty as the first Angela but he liked everything about her. She was a nice girl, a good girl, who made him laugh a lot but who had to tell him more than once to keep his hands…uh, hand to himself (until she was ready). He didn't mind. He could wait. No, he didn't mind that a bit. Not one bit.

Thank you for taking the time to read Palette of the Improbable. If you enjoyed it, please consider telling your friends or posting a short review on Amazon.com. Word of mouth is an author's best friend and much appreciated.

Thank you, Steve Vasquez.

About the Author

Steve Vasquez was born in San Antonio, Texas. He has a B.A. in Communications & a B.A. in English and lives in San Diego with his wife, daughter and cat.

Made in the USA
Charleston, SC
16 March 2017